At Ease

At
Ease

Jeff Ross

ORCA BOOK PUBLISHERS

Library and Archives Canada Cataloguing in Publication

Ross, Jeff, 1973–, author
At ease / Jeff Ross.
(Orca limelights)

Issued in print and electronic formats.
ISBN 978-1-4598-0800-3 (pbk.).—ISBN 978-1-4598-0801-0 (pdf).—
ISBN 978-1-4598-0802-7 (epub)

I. Title. II. Series: Orca limelights
PS8635.06928A82 2015   jc813'.6   C2015-901724-6
C2015-901725-4

First published in the United States, 2015
Library of Congress Control Number: 2015935528

Summary: Will has the talent required for a career as a
classical violinist, but stage fright threatens to destroy his dream.

*Orca Book Publishers is dedicated to preserving the environment and has
printed this book on Forest Stewardship Council® certified paper.*

Orca Book Publishers gratefully acknowledges the support for
its publishing programs provided by the following agencies:
the Government of Canada through the Canada Book Fund and the
Canada Council for the Arts, and the Province of British Columbia
through the BC Arts Council and the Book Publishing Tax Credit.

Cover design by Rachel Page
Cover photography by Getty Images

ORCA BOOK PUBLISHERS
www.orcabook.com

Printed and bound in Canada.

18 17 16 15 • 4 3 2 1

For Luca, the first person to read these pages and a source of endless inspiration.

To play a wrong note is insignificant; to play without passion is inexcusable.
—Ludwig van Beethoven

One

I played the final note of the sonata, letting the sound ring for an eternity.

My teacher, Mr. Jorgensen, laughed and said, "Again."

"What was wrong?"

"Nothing. It was perfect. Well, not perfect. It's music, so it can never be perfect. Perfect in music means those little robots who play every note for exactly the right length of time and with absolutely no feeling whatsoever. No, that was quintessential, William. That was...stunning. Play it again!"

"There's nothing I could do better?"

Mr. Jorgensen's fist flew to his lips as he began hacking, almost doubling over. He held a hand up as we waited for the attack to end. "Nothing," he said. "Except doing it again. Entirely for my amusement."

I placed my violin back in its spot. Set my chin on the rest. The rough, worn skin there burned a little.

And I played.

The piece was Bach's Sonata No. 1 in G Minor—Presto. It's written for solo violin, and it moves so quickly that it proves practicing scales is never a waste of time. Run after run, your fingers need to fly to make it sound right. It's the kind of piece where, once you're done, people might marvel at how you were able to memorize all the notes, never mind play them. But for me, it was a fairly boring, straightforward piece that lacked any real personality.

And yet I loved it, simply because there was nothing I enjoyed more than playing violin. Nothing in my life came even close to the feeling of my fingers on the strings and the sound of the notes stretching out above me.

I guess you could refer to what Mr. Jorgensen and I did as lessons, but it never really felt that way. He took me on as a student just after I had my fifth birthday. I've been told it began when I heard music coming from his apartment, which is next to my family's. Apparently, I refused to leave his door until my mother knocked and asked what the music was.

That was ten years ago.

I didn't start playing right away. At first, my parents just needed someone to watch me after school, and Mr. Jorgensen agreed to be my baby-sitter as long as we only listened to music—*None of that garbage television stuff*, as he put it. He said I needed to be well versed in all types of music first, and if I still felt a passion for violin, then it was meant to be.

Even though Mr. Jorgensen had been the conductor of a number of orchestras, we listened to everything from Gregorian chants (weird) to Miley Cyrus (seriously? This is music?). We covered soul, country, rock, reggae—even electronic. Always circling back to classical. Once I was certain I didn't want to play the trumpet, or twist knobs on a keyboard, or sing a Justin Bieber song in front of a TV audience, we settled down with the violin.

First the easy pieces, starting with "Twinkle, Twinkle, Little Star" and "Mary Had a Little Lamb."

Mr. Jorgensen would never allow me to move on to another piece until I "felt each and every note." Which, honestly, sounds ridiculous for a song like "The Happy Farmer."

But he was right.

Until I truly felt each note coming out of me, I didn't really enjoy playing. I mean, I liked it. But there were times when I was just playing the notes to get through the song.

Mr. Jorgensen would never stand for this. And somehow he always knew.

I've never had another teacher. Never played for anyone but Mr. Jorgensen and my parents. But for the past ten years, I have spent a minimum of two hours a day focusing on getting better and learning more about the violin.

"And around, yes, Will, yes, now to the end!" Eyes closed, hands together, Mr. Jorgensen seemed more lost in the moment than I was.

I kept playing, feeling the music seep out of me.

"Perfect, perfect," he said. Laughing and clapping his hands as though I were playing some East Coast foot-stomper and not a serious, solo Bach piece.

Bach has never been my favorite, which was why Mr. Jorgensen had me playing this. He said that if I could play a piece I didn't enjoy, imagine what I would be able to do with the ones I loved.

Such as Paganini's Caprice No. 24 in A Minor.

The first time I heard that piece, I thought my head was going to explode. It's everything at once: motion and energy and power. Playing it is like riding a brakeless bicycle down a winding hill. Like being entirely outside of your body and only coming back to the ground when it's over.

Mr. Jorgensen turned in his chair as I was finishing and yelled, "Is that enough for you, Alisha?"

I froze, letting a muddle of notes crash to the floor.

"Alisha?" I said.

Which was when Mr. Jorgensen's daughter stepped out of the kitchen and my entire life changed.

"You were right, Dad," Alisha said.

Alisha hadn't heard me play before, but I'd seen her at Mr. Jorgensen's apartment a few times. She's tall and blond and wears a lot of rings and bracelets. She's my parents' age, I guess. I've heard a lot from Mr. Jorgensen about how she's never given him grandchildren. It's always left me wondering if I'm a substitute grandson for him.

"That isn't even his best piece," Mr. Jorgensen told her. "Far from it."

"How old are you?" Alisha asked me.

"Fifteen?" I said. Like I didn't know the answer.

"*Fifteen,* Dad? *Fifteen!* Why didn't you..."

Mr. Jorgensen pulled himself up in his chair. He tended to sink down in it as I played. "He needed to reach a certain level. I told you this."

"But that piece is well beyond his years. I've never heard—"

"He has more difficult ones in his repertoire. But that one. *That one,*" he said, then collapsed into another coughing fit. "That one is stunning."

"You don't say." She put a hand to her chin and stared at me the way people stare at paintings in the National Gallery.

"The thing is, he hates it." Mr. Jorgensen looked at me. "Don't you, Will?"

I was too busy trying not to be freaked out by Alisha staring at me to respond. "It's not my favorite," I finally managed.

"Have you ever been to the NAC?" Alisha asked. I didn't answer right away, so she said, "The National Arts Centre. Right here in Ottawa."

"Once," I said. "To see James Ehnes."

Her face brightened. "Do you like James?"

"Yes," I said, though not with the enthusiasm I felt. James Ehnes is absolutely the greatest living violinist. He may be the greatest violinist ever, but that's impossible to say because you can't actually see the dead ones play live. Sure, there are *recordings* of live performances, but they aren't even close to the actual performances.

You need to be in the room watching and listening to understand.

"He's very nice," Alisha said. "And very good."

"Exquisite," Mr. Jorgensen said. "James feels every note. Just like Will here. He inhales the music, then releases it as if it has never been played before."

"He was at Meadowmount at your age," Alisha said. She seemed to be talking to herself. Her rings shone in the late-afternoon light seeping through the bay window.

"So," Mr. Jorgensen asked. "You'll be accepting him to your school, of course."

7

"I'll need his parents to fill out the registration forms. And I'll need a recording. But when the others hear this..."

Mr. Jorgensen stood and did something on his laptop. "I recorded today," he said. "You'll have to edit it. Don't use the last one—I might have talked a little during it."

"You think?" Alisha said, shaking her head at her father before looking to me. "Is that okay?"

"Is what okay?" I had no idea what was going on. It was just a Tuesday practice at the beginning of summer vacation. I had been with Mr. Jorgensen all day. We had walked around the park by the canal in the morning, fed the ducks, had a hot dog and Fanta for lunch, and been practicing in his apartment ever since.

"He didn't tell you?" Alisha said.

"I didn't want to frighten him," Mr. Jorgensen replied.

"Dad! You told me we were just doing a blind audition."

Mr. Jorgensen waved her concerns away again. "So blind he didn't even know you were in the apartment. It was the only way, Alisha."

It seemed as if she was about to scold her father again, but instead she turned back to me. "I'm sorry about that. I would never have listened in without your permission."

"That's okay," I said, though it felt strange. I didn't know whether to be angry or embarrassed, especially since I didn't feel I'd been playing all that well.

"I coordinate the Young Musicians program at the university. It's a two-week summer workshop for the very best young musicians in Canada. You work with our professionals on your instrument. You practice two or three hours a day, and you take seminars, master classes and private lessons. Does that sound like fun?"

"I guess." I wasn't even certain what all those things were. Seminars? Master classes? Practicing two or three hours a day was something I already did, so that didn't faze me.

Alisha laughed. "He guesses. Dad, where have you been keeping this kid?"

"Under a rock and away from you people just long enough that he knows what he knows and no one will be able to ruin it."

"We don't ruin anything, Dad." She crossed the room to stand before me.

"Sure you don't," Mr. Jorgensen said. "You *prepare* them."

"This could be quite the big step for you," she said, ignoring him. "There will be representatives there from a number of universities, and from The Juilliard School for the performing arts."

"Okay."

"James Ehnes went to Juilliard. He says it's where he truly began to understand his instrument. Do you think you're ready?"

"I guess."

Mr. Jorgensen stood and grabbed me by the shoulders. "Will. This is your shot. You impress those people and you've written your ticket. You will perform all over the world. These are the gatekeepers."

"Not quite, Dad," Alisha said.

"As close as it gets," he said. "Without some kind of backing, you'll become a brilliant unknown."

Alisha turned to me. "Would you like to work with us, Will?" she asked. "Would you like to come to the summer program and play violin every day with some of the best musicians in the country? Would you like to take the next step toward a career in music?"

I looked at Mr. Jorgensen.

"Absolutely," he said. "It is time."

Two

"You have to get Wolski," a girl said. "If you play cello, you need Mr. Wolski."

"I have Abrams," a girl cradling a cello said.

We were in a lecture hall at the university on the first day of the summer program. I sat down away from everyone else, and three girls decided to sit near me and then immediately pretend I didn't exist. It seemed as if a lot of the kids already knew one another, though there were a few like me scattered among the clusters—wide-eyed kids sitting alone, clutching their instruments.

"Mrs. Abrams?" the girl barked. "Mrs. Abrams shouldn't even be here. She's never *really* played. She's never done any solo work. She's never even been in a professional orchestra. I have no idea where she trained. Probably just at a university somewhere out west." The girl crossed her arms and shook her head. "I mean, why bother?"

"Oh," the cellist said. She looked back at the schedule in front of her. "I have her for two sessions."

"*Two* sessions?" It seemed like the first girl, a skinny redhead with a violin resting on her lap, was going to lose her mind. Instead, she just shrugged and gave the cellist a pitying look.

"Do you have Wolski?" the girl sitting next to me asked the redhead. She had thick brown hair and chestnut eyes. When she caught me glancing at her, she shot me a quick smile.

"I play violin," the redhead said, holding up her instrument. "So, obviously, I have Powell. If you play violin, you absolutely have to have Powell."

"Okay," the brunette said. She turned to me, raised her eyebrows in an exaggerated motion and mouthed "Wow."

"How do you know all this?" the cellist asked.

"This is my third time here," the redhead said. "And this is my year. The Juilliard people are going to be snatching up the best of us. I intend to blow their minds." She nodded as though agreeing with herself. "Juilliard is where I belong."

Alisha walked onto the stage. It made me feel a little more secure seeing her there. I barely knew her, but we'd talked a lot since she'd asked me to join the program. There were forms to complete, questions to answer, permissions to be given. My parents were thrilled for me. And eventually, I started to see what it was I'd signed up for.

The weird thing was that I'd never thought about where all the practice was taking me, which might sound stupid—I don't know. I am fifteen though. I kind of doubt anyone at fifteen really has a clear picture of how they'll spend the rest of their life. You practice something and get good at it because you love doing it. It never really feels like work. It doesn't feel like something you need to do to *get* somewhere. I couldn't imagine ever not playing.

As Alisha had explained it, this program was a giant stepping stone to greater things. *You could be the next James Ehnes,* she'd said.

Which, to me, meant I could do nothing but play violin all the time. I didn't hate school, though I could do without all the tests we were forced to take. I liked some of the English courses, but that was because we were just reading books. My school didn't have a music program, so that wasn't even an option. Every day was kind of the same. I spent my time waiting to get back to Mr. Jorgensen's apartment to practice.

This program, once I began to understand it, felt like a gift. Before I even went in that first day, I knew Alisha was right. I needed this.

I wanted it.

Up on the stage, Alisha clapped her hands to get our attention. "Hello, everyone, and welcome," she said. "It's nice to see so many familiar faces. And just as many new ones. I'm very excited for this year to begin." There were some cheers and clapping, and then Alisha went on to talk about the program. The two weeks we would have at the university. How we would be working with some of the very best musicians in the area. And then she dropped an absolute bomb.

"It is also a great honor for me to announce," she said, stopping and looking out at the audience over her glasses, "that violinist James Ehnes will be joining us for a master class on the final day of our program."

I almost dropped my violin. It was in its case, but still.

"He will work with five students individually," Alisha said after the muttering and muffled clapping ceased. "I know there are more than five violinists here, so this will be a difficult decision to make. Luckily, James has invited us all to his performance at Chamberfest on Thursday night. And he will do a Q & A, so everyone will be able to gain valuable insights from one of our country's most accomplished musicians."

I set my violin down because I didn't trust my hands. They were suddenly sweaty and shaking.

"As some of you have heard, two representatives from Juilliard will be here with us as well. Though they haven't signed on to do any specific sessions, they'll be watching all of the students to see how we do things here. Now, give yourselves a big round of applause because each and every one of you has made it this far, which is, in and of itself, a huge accomplishment."

Everyone began clapping.

Everyone, that is, but me. I just stared at Alisha. She was smiling and clapping along with the crowd. In that moment she reminded me of her father, and I felt a little more comfortable. I grabbed my violin and hugged it to my chest.

"We have twenty minutes before the first session begins," Alisha said. "If you see someone you haven't met, introduce yourself. There are volunteers in the hallway who can help you with directions. Enjoy!"

The brunette girl turned to me with her hand outstretched. "I'm Danielle," she said.

"Will." I shook her hand.

"How old are you?"

"Fifteen," I said.

She wrinkled her forehead at me. "But you need to be sixteen to be here, right?" She tapped the redhead's shoulder. "Don't you need to be sixteen to be here?"

"Of course," the redhead said. "Why?"

"He's fifteen," Danielle said.

"Do you turn sixteen this week or something?"

"No," I said. "I actually just turned fifteen." I had no idea there was an age requirement for the program.

Alisha was walking past, and the redhead called to her, "Miss Jorgensen!"

Alisha stopped and leaned against a seat. "Yes, Cathy?"

"This boy says he's fifteen."

Alisha looked at me for a moment. "Don't you worry about that," she said.

"But you need to be sixteen!" Cathy said.

Alisha looked at Cathy's schedule. "I see you have Mr. Powell this year. You should be very happy about that, Cathy."

"Of course I am."

"I'm certain he'll help you a great deal." Alisha carried on up the walkway and out the door.

Cathy turned back to me. "Are you sure you're only fifteen?"

"Yeah," I said. It was a really stupid question. As if I'd momentarily forgotten how old I was.

She shook her head. "Who do you have for your sessions?"

I hadn't looked at my schedule yet. Just being in that massive room had been enough to put me on edge. I pulled the folded sheet from my backpack. There was a piece of tape holding the edges together. I started working on it with my thumbnail. Before I could get the tape off, the sheet was yanked from my hand.

I looked up to find Cathy ripping the tape off and flicking the schedule open.

"Powell," she said. She narrowed her eyes at me, then turned to Danielle. "He must be special." She looked back at me. "Are you special?"

I had no idea how to answer, so I didn't say anything.

Cathy stood and held my schedule out toward me. Before I could get my hand on it, she let it drop. "I guess we'll see," she said. Then she slipped out the end of the aisle, taking the cellist with her.

Danielle picked up my schedule and looked at it. "We both have group performance first," she said. "I think I know where the room is, if you want to go together." She had her violin case in one hand and a bag over her other shoulder.

I wiped my hands on my jeans and grabbed my violin and backpack.

We moved down the aisle to the walkway. She opened the door for me, and as I passed through, she asked, "So *are* you special?"

Three

There were names taped to the backs of all the seats in the room. Three groupings of four chairs. I found my name right next to Danielle's. Two other people, an Asian girl and a guy with perfectly round glasses, were already in their seats. The guy had shifted forward and seemed on the verge of speaking when a man at the front of the room clapped his hands, then raised his arms above his head.

"Hello, hello, all. Take your seats, please. For those who don't know me, I am Charles Powell." He moved to the right side of the room and stood before a tall white screen.

I'd never seen anyone so elegantly dressed this early in the day: black suit, black tie, shiny black shoes. His hair was parted to one side, each strand settled exactly where, I assumed, it always was.

He held his hands in front of him and scanned the room, seeming to take in each person as he spoke.

"We will begin with a simple task. Look around you at the people in your cluster. This is the quartet in which you will perform. I would like each of you to tell one another three things. Your name, your instrument and your favorite piece to play. Nothing more, nothing less." He held his hands up. "You have ten minutes."

The girl across from me spoke immediately, as though she simply had to get out whatever it was she needed to say and then sink back into the safety of silence. "I am Olivia Chang. I play the viola. My favorite piece is anything by Mozart." She didn't smile. Didn't react in any way at all to what she had just said. She inhaled deeply, then exhaled at the same rate and nodded in agreement with herself.

"Anything specific by Mozart?" Danielle asked.

Olivia had her dark black hair pulled tightly behind her head, which made her gray eyes stand out all the more. "Just anything," she said.

We waited a moment for something more before the boy jumped in. "My name's Jon and I hate talking to people, but what can you do, right? You have to live in this crazy world, and if interacting with other people is what has to happen, then whatever. I don't know what I'm talking about, so don't even listen. But I play the cello because my parents think I should. Like, my mother played when she was younger but wasn't great, and my father thinks it's better to play an instrument rather than, like, *Call of Duty*, and I don't even get a vote on that matter. And my favorite piece to play is anything Yo-Yo Ma has not played, because he's a hack."

"Wow," Danielle said when Jon finished. And I had to agree. Wow. I didn't think he'd taken a breath the entire time. I felt like a stiff, angry wind had passed through me.

"If you don't like playing, why are you here?" Olivia said.

"Well, it's not like I hate it, it's just that there are so many other things to do, you know? And I guess I'm good at it. It's easy, right? You just play the notes."

"It is *not* easy," Danielle said. She put a hand over her mouth. "Sorry. I'm Danielle, or just Dani. I play violin. And stringed instruments are not easy for me. Maybe they are for you, but for me the violin is incredibly difficult. As for a specific piece, I have always been amazed by—"

"Maybe *4'33"*," Jon suddenly interrupted.

Dani looked at him with narrowed eyes. "What?"

"John Cage. The one that's four minutes and thirty-three seconds of silence. That's probably my favorite piece to perform."

"You don't *perform* that," Olivia said.

"You do. It's art." Jon laughed, a quick snort.

"As I was saying, I could listen to Shostakovich all day, but I doubt I'd ever be able to play anything. Not well enough anyway." Dani pointed at me.

"Um, Will?" I said. I held up my case. "Violin? And Paganini."

"Oh, we have a rock star in our midst," Jon said.

"Sorry?"

"Paganini? He's, like, the rock star of classical music. All that flashy stuff with the runs and the double stops and how fast it all is."

"Okay," I said.

"So you admit it," Jon said.

"What?"

"You're a rock star!" He laughed.

I just stared at him.

"I'm kidding." He put his arms on the back of his chair. "We're not rock stars." He shook his head. "We're classical musicians, a dying breed at best."

Olivia inhaled and exhaled again. "Are we done?"

"I guess so," Dani said.

"Good," Olivia said, pulling her cell phone out.

Mr. Powell clapped his hands. "That's time," he said. "I hope you all had a chance to get to know one another, because it's time to get to work. You'll find music on the stand before you. Go ahead and take a look."

I turned the sheets over to find Mozart's Adagio and Fugue in C Minor.

"Not very imaginative," Olivia said, going back to her phone.

Mr. Powell clapped his hands again. "Now that you see your piece, you'll know you have been put into groups for a specific reason. I diligently listened to your audition tapes and have placed you each with people of, I hope, like mind and ability."

We all looked at one another.

Right away I found myself wondering if Jon would pull his weight. If Olivia would be able to set her phone down long enough to practice.

Most of all, I wondered which of us, Dani or I, would get to take the first violin part.

"Go ahead and start," Mr. Powell said.

"I did this last year," Olivia said. "The Fugue part is more interesting. Should we start with it?"

"Sure," Danielle said.

The whole room filled with music as everyone bowed at once. Jon plowed his way through the first dozen or so bars as if he were working on an assembly line. Olivia rushed through the first sheet of the viola part with the clipped perfection of someone who had played it so often that it had become the soundtrack to her dreams.

"Have you played this before?" Danielle asked me.

"A few times," I said. "But only with a recording."

"You play the first violin, okay?"

I nodded and brought my violin to my chin.

We managed to get through the first page before Mr. Powell was standing over us, his arms in the air.

"Okay, quiet, everyone," he said. "We'll start with this group here. If you could please sight-read the first sheet for us. Have you decided who will be the first violin?"

"Will," Dani said.

Mr. Powell looked at me. Up close, he seemed even more well put together. His shirt was wrinkle free, his tie tightly clasped to his shirt with a golden clip.

"So you are Will Neises." A crinkle appeared at the right side of his mouth. "Okay, let's give it a try."

It was then that I noticed everyone watching me. Dani and Olivia had their backs to the rest of the room, Mr. Powell was off to one side, and Jon was right next to me. So when I set my violin back in place, it felt as though everyone was staring directly at me.

I looked at the music.

But not really.

I mean, I was looking at the music, but I couldn't really see it. The notes were blurry.

Jon tapped his foot a couple of times, then played the first note. Olivia and Dani jumped in immediately, leaving me staring at the fuzzy page.

"Together," Mr. Powell said. He tapped my music stand with his baton. "Start again." He cupped his chin and looked down at me.

There was something wrong with my stomach. It felt like someone had sent an eviction notice there and the contents were getting restless and angry. There was a strange ringing in my ears. Like little bells accompanied by a high-pitched squeal.

I shook my head and almost dropped my bow, my fingers were so sweaty.

I'd been forced to do things in front of people before. Presentations in school, for instance. Once, I had to hand out the awards at an assembly. I mean, I knew what nerves were. But I'd never played the violin in front of anyone but Mr. Jorgensen and, occasionally, my parents.

I wasn't ready for this.

Jon pulled the first note again. Dani and Olivia jumped in. I put my bow down too quickly and forced a screech from the instrument. A couple of people jumped in their seats.

Jon laughed.

"Sorry," he said. "Are you okay? You've kind of turned red."

"What?" I said. Everyone was melting in and out of focus, like the space right above the pavement on a hot summer day.

"You have," Dani whispered. "Are you allergic to something?"

"Try again," Mr. Powell said.

I glanced at him. His face suddenly seemed larger. He flicked his sleeve up and glanced at his watch. The ticking of that watch beat in my ears. The steady, slow falling away of time. It wasn't moving quickly enough, though, because I was still sitting there and everyone was still waiting.

I tried to breathe, but that felt impossible.

I'd already screwed up. Apparently, my head looked like it was going to explode. The notes were still a blur on the page before me.

Everyone was watching me.

I could see the redhead, Cathy, whispering behind her hand to her friend. She moved her hand away to reveal a knowing smirk.

"Sorry," I said. "I'm...I think I need to go to the bathroom."

"Try the first line, Will," Mr. Powell said, his voice suddenly reverberating around the room.

"No. I mean, I need to..." I got up, knocking the music stand as I did so. I felt hot and damp. Also like my legs weren't attached. I was just this big red head floating toward the back of the room.

"Leave your violin..." I heard someone say behind me. But I was already gone. Out the door and into the hallway. I stumbled past a dozen doors before I saw the little man symbol and bashed through, almost dropping my violin on the tiled floor.

I went into a stall, sat down on the toilet seat and breathed in the foul bathroom stink. But even that didn't matter, because I was completely alone. No one was watching me.

"What the hell?" I said to the empty stall. "I mean, seriously, what the hell?"

Four

"Tell me all about it," Mr. Jorgensen said when I returned home that night. "I want to hear everything."

He was outside our apartment building, sitting on a lawn chair we kept on the porch. His big smile shone up at me. I sat on the railing and went through the whole day: the group class, the private practice session and the end-of-day meet and greet. I left out the part where I lost my mind.

A bus stopped outside, releasing people from another workday. They all seemed so tired and worn. My mother exited last. She came up the steps and inspected me with her red eyes. She worked for the government as an office manager, and it seemed as though every day was more difficult than the one before.

"How did it go?" she said. It was humid, as Ottawa often is, and her hair was all puffy.

"Great," I replied. I already knew that these stories wouldn't hold up. Alisha would have heard what had happened, and she'd eventually pass it on to her father. There could very well be a message on his answering machine already.

"Good." She pushed her hair from her face. "Is your father home?"

"I don't know," I said. "I haven't been up yet."

She opened the door and stepped inside. "I'll get supper going." And then she was gone.

"That was only the first day," Mr. Jorgensen said. "There is so much for you to learn." He grabbed my arm. "You need to blow those Juilliard people away, Will. They are your ticket." He kept biting his lower lip, and there was a shake to his head that I'd never seen before. "I've helped you as much as I can. Now you have to go out into that world and perform. Play your heart out."

I'd spent the entire afternoon feeling like a complete loser. I knew I could play the piece, yet in that moment I'd been unable to move. Nothing like that had ever happened to me before. But then, I'd never had to play in front of an audience before. It was as if my mind no longer controlled my body. My hands wouldn't stop shaking, and my eyes couldn't focus; I hadn't even been able to hear properly.

"I worried that keeping you away from performing was a mistake," Mr. Jorgensen said. "That maybe you should do more with others. But I think we made the right decision all along."

* * *

After dinner, I sat down with the music and played through it five times without a hitch. I put my violin away that night thinking the next day would be easy. That what had happened to me had been a fluke. Too much to take in at once.

Or maybe it was a bad bagel or something at breakfast.

Whatever it was, it wouldn't happen again. I hoped.

In bed that night, I rolled so much that my sheets were wrapped around me as though I were a mummy. In the morning, I ached. Not my muscles though.

Something else entirely.

Something I'd never even considered before.

Something sunk so deep inside me, I had no idea it was even there.

Fear of failure.

Five

"So, is he special?" Cathy asked Dani.

We were all standing around in the cafeteria, eating donuts and drinking orange juice.

"Who?" Dani said.

"Him," Cathy said, pointing at me.

"I don't know," Dani said. She smiled at me and raised her eyebrows.

"What was with the freak-out yesterday?" Cathy said, suddenly addressing me.

"I think I ate something bad," I lied.

"Sure you did."

"It was the first appearance of Hulk-Aid," Jon said.

We all looked at him and waited.

"Like, Will's superhero personality," he said. "A combination of the Hulk and the Kool-Aid Man. Hulk-Aid. Instead of turning green, he turns red. And then he destroys walls and stuff. But it doesn't happen when he's angry, it happens when he's nervous. It's literally terrifying."

"Um, okay," Cathy said, then fake shivered. "These are your people?" she said to Dani.

"Yes. These are my people."

"Well, good luck with that." Cathy walked away, leaving an almost perceptible fog of self-righteousness in her wake.

"What's up her butt?" Jon asked.

Olivia, for once without her nose touching her cell screen, said, "She's being realistic."

"How so?"

"She knows that this is super important. Like, Juilliard people are going to be here. Can you imagine going to Juilliard? Everyone who comes out of there has a career. They have the best teachers on the planet. There is no better place for creative people. I intend to apply there for grad school."

"So because everything is competitive, she has to be an idiot? I don't understand the relationship," Jon said, pumping his arms and talking like a robot. "Does not compute."

"You're the idiot if you don't see it," Olivia said. Her phone buzzed and she glanced at it, then back at us. "Did you all practice the Adagio last night?"

"Nope," Jon said.

"A little," Dani said.

"Sure," I said.

Olivia's phone buzzed again, and she walked away staring at it.

"We have Powell for the whole morning," Dani said, looking at the schedule. "You going to be all right?"

"I'll be fine," I said.

Jon picked up his cello. "Sure you will be, buddy," he said. "You just got to turn your Hulk-Aid rage into a perfect performance."

"That's not going to catch on," Dani said.

"What, Hulk-Aid?"

"Yeah."

"Sure it will. It's gold," Jon said. "Pure gold."

As we walked to our practice room, Jon kept talking. "I mean, everyone gets nervous," he said.

"Uh-huh."

"Maybe not everyone. Like, I don't. Not really. But that's because I don't care what happens. Like, if I mess up, I mess up. Maybe that's what you need to do. Stop caring."

"Quit it with that," Dani said. "You care. I can tell."

"I don't. I really don't. It has kept me invincible."

"I don't get you," Dani said to Jon.

"No one does," Jon said. "No one ever will."

"If you don't want to be here, then why are you? It's not like you just pay and you're in. You have to apply and send a recording in and be accepted. It is crazy competitive."

"I'm naturally talented," he said. "And terminally lazy."

"So I guess you understand yourself pretty well," Dani said.

"It is what it is. I was born with a talent." He held his fingers up. "There's magic in these here digits. But here," he said, tapping his chest, "there is love only for the vids. Television. Flickering lights and pretty colors."

Dani shook her head. "I don't buy it. You wouldn't be here if you didn't want to be."

"There you are wrong. I don't have a choice. Plus, when you think about it, playing an instrument in, like, an orchestra or something is a pretty easy gig. No cubicles. No math. No early mornings but plenty of late nights. That's not a half-bad life. So until I can get paid for playing *Call of Duty*, it is with the cello I shall suffer."

I didn't believe Jon either. And I didn't know why he was trying to pretend he didn't care about cello. I mean, I'd watched him play.

He went to another place when he started bowing.

We caught up to Olivia, and she raised her eyes from her phone to take me in. "You just need to relax," she said. "Breathe. Focus. That's the most important thing. Focus."

"You're good," Dani said. "Just make certain you know your piece. That it's as perfect as it can get. That's what I do. I keep practicing until it plays in my head when I go to sleep at night. Until it's the first thing I hear when I wake up. It's the only way to do it."

"Okay," I said. I wanted them to shut up, because the more they talked about being nervous, the more nervous I became.

Dani and Olivia cut into the girls' washroom as we were heading toward our practice room. Which was when Jon decided to say, "She's amazing."

"Who?" I replied.

"Olivia," he said. "Wait—you're not into her, are you?"

"What?"

"Because I looked her up online last night. I found her Facebook page and Instagram. She started something on Pinterest but I guess got bored with that."

"What are you talking about?"

"She likes all these obscure books and the *Matrix* movies, but also *Legally Blonde* and *Frozen.* So complicated. Her music isn't just classical either. She likes some Swedish hip-hop. Did you even know that existed? I listened to some. It's shocking. She also says she runs and would like to learn to longboard, but I have a feeling that was all about this guy on her Facebook page, because he left a comment that said *Cool, would love to teach you,* but there's no chance for that romance because honestly, how deep can a love of skateboarding really go?"

"You're talking about Olivia?"

"Yes. Keep up, man."

We found our practice room. Jon stepped in first. "Not bad, not bad," he said.

A bank of windows on the southern wall was open, letting in the fresh beginnings of summer. Music stands had been arranged in front of four chairs. Jon went to the two chairs where he and Olivia would be sitting and shifted them slightly closer together. A moment later Olivia and Dani came in. Olivia moved her seat away from Jon's, then got out her viola, set it on her lap and went back to texting or whatever it was she was doing on her phone.

"You do the first part, okay?" Dani said when we were all set up. "I've only practiced the second."

"Okay," I said. "Should we do the Adagio?"

"Let's try the Fugue again," Dani said.

And just like that, we began.

And it was amazing.

Other than when Mr. Jorgensen accompanied me on the piano, I'd never played with anyone else. We made it about halfway through before Olivia slipped up. She'd already missed a couple of bars, but this time she dropped her bow as she was turning the page.

We ground to a halt.

"Sorry," Olivia said as she picked up her bow.

"Wow," Dani said. She poked me. "You *are* special."

"Is that the only piece you have ever played?" Jon asked.

"No," I said.

"Because if I practiced this one piece every day for, like, years, I might sound something like that. Only on cello. Forget the violin—I don't know how you people get your fingers in the right spots on those little fingerboards." He laughed and shook his head. "Boggles the mind. Same with viola. And what if you have fat fingers?" He looked at Olivia. "I'm not saying you have fat fingers and that's what happened to you there. I mean, I don't think you have fat anything, not that I'm..."

"Do you want to start from where we left off?" Dani said, saving Jon.

"That sounds like an awesome idea," Jon said.

We readied our instruments and began to play. It took a couple of bars to get back in sync, but when we did, it really sounded awesome. I was smiling as I played. I could feel it in my cheeks. I looked to Jon, who smiled back, and to Olivia, who, amazingly, was beaming. Her face looked entirely different with the giant smile. She looked brighter and, for once, as though she was enjoying herself rather than analyzing everything that was happening around her.

Most important, I didn't feel nervous at all. Not even slightly. The music just rose up through me and flowed out easily.

We came to the end of the Fugue at almost a whisper.

"Bravo!"

We turned to find Mr. Powell standing at the doorway, clapping madly.

"Incredible. Now the Adagio."

My back was to the door, so when I turned around, all I could see was the side of Dani's face and Olivia sitting bolt upright, bow posed over her viola.

"We're really trying to nail the Fugue first, Mr. Powell," Olivia said.

"Fine. Play it again then. I missed the beginning."

It took us a few bars to really get together, but once we were going it was, again, amazing.

And still I felt fine. Absolutely fine. My fingers hit where they were supposed to. My bow was steady and loose.

When we finished, I felt Mr. Powell's hand on my shoulder.

"Extraordinary," he said. "Alisha was right."

I didn't look up, but I could feel his eyes on my head.

"Will we be performing this for the final concert?" Olivia asked.

"Absolutely," Mr. Powell said. He returned to the doorway. "The Juilliard people will love it. I guarantee it. Run through it a couple more times. You four have the recording studio for the rest of the day." And with that he was gone.

Olivia immediately picked up her phone.

"Well, this is good," Jon said.

"Why?" Dani asked.

"Because we've already nailed it." He looked over at Olivia. "Seriously, what are you looking at on that thing?"

"I just wanted to be certain we would be performing this piece before I showed you *this*."

"What?" Jon said, leaning closer. "And how does looking at your phone tell you anything about us?"

"It doesn't tell me anything about us at all." Olivia held her phone up.

"What is that?"

"The cover for Yo-Yo Ma's recording of Adagio and Fugue in C Minor."

"What? No!"

"That's right. Yo-Yo."

Jon cringed and buried his head in his hands.

Six

L unch was held in a large hall. Sandwiches, salads, pickles and bottles of juice and pop. By the end of the first half hour, nothing remained but tomato juice and potato salad, circled by twisted napkins and little mounds of pepper.

We sat around the circumference of the room, cross-legged and sticking almost entirely to our ensemble groups. Olivia disappeared at first, hovering around a few other people, always standing and looking down at them with cell phone in hand, then finally returned to us, sliding down the wall to sit beside Dani.

"Hey, Will?" Jon said.

"Yeah?" I hadn't been in a ton of social situations, but something about Jon's tone left me feeling I was being set up.

"What are your thoughts on Timbuktu?"

"The place or..."

"The Swedish hip-hop artist." Jon looked directly at Olivia as he said this. She may have twitched a little. Not much, but there was a brief moment when her attention was diverted from whatever was on her tiny screen.

"I've never heard his work," I said.

Having nowhere to go, Jon managed, "Well, it's pretty cool. I mean, I love it. I've been into the whole Swedish hip-hop scene for a few years. The beats are *intense*." He continued to look at Olivia, waiting for her response. When none came, he shrugged, discouraged.

I felt I should add something to the conversation to help him out, but I had no idea what.

"Who have you been working with?" Dani asked me between bites of her sandwich.

"Oh, just this guy in my apartment building."

"You're not with a studio?"

"No, this is the first time I've ever really played with anyone else."

"Who is this guy? I want to train with him."

"His name is Mr. Jorgensen."

"Like Alisha?" Olivia said, finally glancing away from her electronic world.

"Yeah, he's her dad."

"Well, that explains it," said a familiar voice.

I looked up to find Cathy standing over me.

"Hey, Cathy," Dani said.

"You're not just special," Cathy said. "You're also a favorite. This is, like, nepotism. It also explains why you're on the performance list today." I had no idea what she was talking about. "You're becoming the whole school's pet, aren't you? Miss Jorgensen brought you in here. You're her dad's little prodigy. I've already heard Powell going on about you."

"No one said he was a prodigy," Dani said.

"They will. But wait a second—only if they get to hear you perform. And that's not likely to happen, now is it?"

"No one's performing today," Jon said.

"*Au contraire*, my four-eyed friend. Every day, three people perform in front of the entire group. They say the people are randomly selected, but he's on today with Sung and Elliott, so they *obviously* are already choosing their favorites," Cathy said.

"What are you talking about?" Dani said.

"The teachers. They all have their favorites. And Will must be Powell's. The Juilliard people are going to be here today as well."

"We have to play in front of everyone?" I said. Already, it felt like my stomach was ready to reject the egg-salad sandwich I'd just eaten—which, obviously, was the worst choice for someone worried about nerves. You just never know with mayonnaise.

"Um, yeah. It's called performing." Cathy shrugged. "I guess with you it'll just be a different kind of entertainment for the rest of us." I thought she was going to walk away, but she just stood there, like she didn't know where else she belonged. "Do you think you could throw up for us? That would be epic." She pulled her cell out. "I'll be recording for posterity."

Then she spotted someone across the room and marched off as though she'd just made some kind of grand statement.

"Did you guys know about this?" I said.

"I knew they did it," Dani said. "I didn't know they'd start on the second day."

"That does seem really soon."

"But they're only doing three a day," Olivia said. "So it'll take the rest of the week to get through everyone."

"What time is this supposed to be happening?" I said.

"It'll be okay, Will," Dani said. She put a hand on my forearm. "Just get up and play something."

"No, I know, it'll be fine. I mean, I'm just trying to figure out when it will happen and what I'm supposed to play and..."

"Chill out, Hulk-Aid."

"Don't call him that, Jon," Dani said.

The buzzing in my ears had returned. I could feel my body vibrating. Already I was inhaling in short gasps.

"Here's the thing about this place," Dani said. "They expect that they're teaching you to be a performer. Like, to be a professional. So just get up and play something you already know by heart. Something you've practiced a lot. It'll be fine."

It wouldn't be fine.

I mean, I knew that was a negative way to think, but my body was telling me it wasn't going to be fine. I felt clammy and shaky and I didn't even know when I was going to have to do this thing.

The next time I looked up, Mr. Powell was standing above us.

"Will, have you heard about your performance this afternoon?" he said, as though it were already done.

"Just kind of."

He crouched and put a hand on my shoulder. "We're hoping you'll play something you know well. Something in the three-minute range."

"Where? Why?"

"Oh, it's something we like to do here to get everyone ready to perform. You'll be announced and then you can come out, bow, tell us what you will be performing, play your piece, bow and be done. It's an opportunity for the students to hear one another."

"I don't want to," I said. And I really, *really* didn't want to. It already felt as if everyone was watching me.

Staring.

Waiting for me to screw up or freak out.

To fail.

"It'll be fine, Will. You need to be able to perform in front of people. That's what you're here for." He shook me a little. "Trial by fire, son. You'll be great."

I was about to respond, to tell him again that I couldn't do it. That I had nothing prepared or felt ill or had an unfortunate paper cut *right on my index finger*, but he'd already patted my shoulder and walked away.

"You're his boyo," Jon said.

I stared blankly at him. "What?"

"Every one of these teachers has a horse in this race, you know? Like, next year one of them will be able to come back and say, 'Oh, did I mention, that student of mine from last year, Will Neises, well, he has gone on to *Juuui*lliard.' And everyone will have to be all super impressed with them, and then that year whoever that teacher is—and I guess if you can pull it together that'll be Powell—will be the superstar. The *best* teacher *evah*. Like it had anything to do with him."

"I...I..." I didn't even know what I was going to say.

Then Jon leaned back, hands in front of his face, and said, "Look out, everyone. Hulk-Aid will erupt in ten, nine, eight..."

Seven

Elliott played like a man possessed.

It was ridiculous.

I'd seen him around but never spoken to him. He was small and quiet, but when he got up on that stage he was a different person.

He seemed to grow.

To expand.

What confused me most was how he could be so calm about it. Playing in front of all these people, his soul completely exposed.

He played the opening of Mendelssohn's Violin Concerto in E Minor. Some of the other students knew the piece and were humming along, anticipating each step. He moved—dipping, shifting from side to side. He wasn't perfect, but he was very, very good. Obviously, he'd practiced this piece. He'd polished all the edges until they shone.

He finished to a round of applause. Whispers of conversation fluttered around me. Some of the kids were talking about how great he was. Others were pointing out small mistakes to their friends. Something *they* might have done better.

Sung got up next and didn't bow or introduce her piece. She just stood there for a few seconds, staring out at the audience. As she brought her bow up, I could see her fingers shaking. She kept sniffing as well, and after playing maybe three bars, she stopped and scratched her nose. Then she started over.

I couldn't tell what Sung was playing. At first I thought it was Mozart, then Bach. It shimmered and wavered in the strangest ways. She seemed to be constantly doubling back on herself. It actually sounded like more than one piece, maybe three or four mashed together. But no one in the audience appeared at all confused. I thought I heard someone else playing as well. A cello rumbling out long, low notes.

Cathy was right in the middle of the crowd, her arms crossed, her eyes on me. On the other wall I could see Mr. Powell. He gave me a flip of his eyebrow, then a thumbs-up.

I leaned toward the stage again, and what I was hearing didn't match the movement of Sung's bow, which was steady and tight. I closed my eyes and felt worse. All the sounds came at once. I exhaled, slowly letting the air out.

What was I doing here? Why was I even bothering? All these people would be staring at me. Judging me. Trying to figure out ways they were better than me. Just waiting for me to fail.

There was no way I would be able to do this. There was that tricky part I'd messed up on before. My hands were sweaty. How was I going to keep my bow steady?

I found that I was tipping, almost falling over. I grabbed my violin at the last second before it slipped from my arm.

I felt Alisha's hand on my shoulder before I saw her or heard her voice.

"Are you okay, Will?"

I shook my head. "I'm really dizzy," I said.

Sung was still on the stage, but she was no longer playing. She was just standing there, her bow in one hand, violin in the other. The audience was clapping. She bowed, and as she left the stage, I could feel everyone looking at me. Whispers flicking through the crowd. Snarling faces exposed for a second before hands went to mouths and secret words were spoken.

Everyone was talking about me.

Everyone was looking at me.

Everyone was waiting for me to perform.

I tried to spot my group, but they were somewhere beyond my vision.

"Can you perform now, Will? Do you feel up to it?"

"I don't know," I said. "I think I ate something bad. My stomach feels awful." I hiccupped and tasted a sampling of the contents of my stomach shooting into my mouth.

"You don't have to perform right now, Will," Alisha said. "It's just a fun thing we do so everyone can get to know one another. So we can all hear one another play."

"Okay."

"It's not a big deal." She rubbed my shoulder, which made me feel even worse. Because now it felt as though everyone was watching me being comforted by Alisha, who, if they wanted to believe it, was the only reason I was even at this school.

"Do you think you can make the afternoon class?" she asked.

"No," I said, dying of embarrassment. "I need to go home."

"Okay, Will. I can take you home," Alisha said.

Mr. Powell was by my side as well. "Are you not going to perform?"

"Not today, Charles," Alisha said.

"We'll get you on the list for tomorrow then," he said, grabbing my arm.

Alisha shot him a look, which I spotted out of the corner of my eye. "Will can perform when he's ready," she said as she walked me from the cafeteria.

*　*　*

When we entered my apartment building, I told Alisha I had to go lie down. She turned to knock on her father's door.

"Can you not tell him?" I said quickly.

"I was going to ask him to look in on you," she said. "Your parents won't be home yet, will they?"

"No, but I'll be fine. I just need to lie down."

"Okay. I might just stop in and say hi though," she said.

"But then he'll ask why you're here and..." I inhaled, my hand on the railing. "I don't want him to worry."

Her eyes dropped and she nodded. "Okay." She took a step toward me, reaching again for my shoulder. But I didn't want to be comforted. I felt like an idiot. And now that I was away from the school, all I wanted to do was go back. To be with everyone else. To get on the stupid stage and play the stupid piece.

"Are you certain you'll be all right?" she asked.

"I really just need to lie down. My parents will be home soon anyway."

"Okay," she said. "We'll see you tomorrow."

I waited and watched her drive away, then went upstairs and lay down on my bed. I knew what was happening to me. I mean, I could tell everyone that it was something I'd eaten. That I had dizzy spells sometimes. I could make up any number of excuses. But in the end, it was pretty simple.

I went to the Internet and searched out stage fright. That's all it was: stage fright.

It happens to everyone, I told myself.

Which, once I started reading, I discovered was entirely true. And it could happen for a million different reasons. Self-confidence cropped up a lot.

As in lack of.

Fear of judgment. Of making a fool of yourself. And, of course, fear of failure.

I began to wonder if Jon had the right attitude. Don't care. Just get up there and do it because it doesn't even matter.

By the time my mother got home, I had confused myself with advice. Meditate, watch something funny, practice the piece to death, breathe, tell yourself you can do it, run up and down stairs, do jumping jacks, imagine your incredible success once you have performed perfectly.

But how could *that* happen? With my sweaty hands and quivering stomach?

"Will, you're home," my mother said, standing in my bedroom doorway.

"Yeah, it ended early today," I lied.

"How was it?"

"Good," I lied again. "Great," said the ultimate lying machine.

She hugged me, holding on for a moment. "I am so proud of you. It's great to see you coming out of your shell." She held me away from her. "You are going to be such a success, Will, I just know it."

The thing was, I hadn't known I had a shell.

And that I hadn't come out of it.

Maybe *that* was the problem. My shell had been broken and all I wanted to do was put it together again so I could crawl back inside.

Forever.

Eight

There were two days of private practice after the incident. Two days where I worked quietly in a room. Talked to Mr. Powell and a couple of other instructors. Two days during which no one asked me to do anything in front of anyone at all.

Two great days.

"You need to adopt my way of thinking," Jon said. It was Friday morning, and we were pawing through the donuts and bagels. There was a carafe of coffee at the end of the table, and some of the kids were filling white cups.

"What way is that?" I said.

"Stop caring," he said. "It makes everything so much easier."

"Will," Olivia said. "First of all, don't listen to him. Second, you know your piece. Pretend those people aren't there. That's my advice. Get up and play and pretend no one is there."

"I felt dizzy before. That's all," I said.

"Sure," Olivia said, bringing out her phone as she stood up. "Don't feel dizzy when *we* perform, all right? My future is on the line too, and, unlike some people, I do think it matters."

"It'll be okay," Dani said, getting to her feet. "Just relax. Just breathe." The two of them left on that note.

And that word rang through my brain: *just*.

What a horrible word. And about as inaccurate as any word can be. Think of the times you use that word. It's *just* another mile. It's *just* a broken heart. It's *just* a scratch.

It's *just* a performance.

"Mr. Neises." Mr. Powell was standing behind me. "I've put you on the performance schedule for the final day. I am sorry you didn't have much time to prepare before. But that tends to be the nature of these performances. They just happen." He smiled. "This time, you will be able to prepare yourself. Would you like to go first?"

"I don't know," I said. Though what I was thinking was, Of course not. There's no way I can do this!

"I'll put you on first." He patted my shoulder. "That will be much easier."

I went to speak, but nothing came out. I knew I couldn't say I would likely eat something bad right before the performance. The only way out of this was to say I was too nervous to play. To explain everything that had been happening to me. To let everyone know I would never be a true performer because I couldn't actually perform.

"Nothing to be nervous about, Will. We're all friends here," he said as he walked away.

Which also wasn't the point. And besides, Mr. Powell was wrong. We weren't all friends.

Cathy had made that abundantly clear. The adults were just too dim to notice.

Jon and I stood up and headed toward the practice room. "So, do you think she likes me?" Jon said.

I stared at him. "Olivia?"

"Olivia, of course. We've already been over this. I thought you might have given my situation a bit of thought."

"I don't know," I said. "Did she catch onto your Swedish hip-hop thing?"

"I tried to talk about it yesterday, but, yeah, after some more research I realized she just got that from some author she likes. It's entirely possible that she has never even listened to any of it. Just hit the thumbs-up. But I feel as though I'm zeroing in on her center."

"Her center?"

"What is at the core of Olivia. Where it is we'll connect."

"Where is that?"

"She seems to be into all this crazy philosophy stuff. Like the meaning of life and the reason we are here."

"Are you sure you have the right person?" I said. Not that I didn't think highly of Olivia. But she didn't seem all that invested in the world, never mind discovering the nature of her existence. Unless, of course, the meaning of life could be found on the tiny screen of a cell phone.

"Yes. Of course I do. So?"

We had arrived at the doorway of the practice room and could see Olivia and Dani setting up inside. "Do I think she likes you?"

"Yeah."

"I have no idea," I said. We stood there for a moment and watched her type away on her phone, never looking up. Not even moving the rest of her body. Just her thumbs.

Jon slowly shook his head. "Man, she is something else."

Nine

"**P**oise," Mr. Powell said.

We were in the lecture hall, and he was, again, on the stage.

"Presence." He made a fist and shook it at us. "Performance. The three Ps." He stood up straight and performed an elaborate, full-bodied bow. As he came back up, he brushed his hair back into place. "Bowing is not the most difficult thing to do. However, if it is done incorrectly, you can appear overly confident or smug. Or, possibly worse, meek. The bow is important, as is the handshake. When you come out from the side of the stage, you must be prepared to shake the first violinist's hand."

He put his hands together in prayer before him. Then, with his right hand, he pointed toward Cathy. "Cathy, could you help me with a demonstration?"

Cathy leaped to her feet and walked with pure determination to the stage.

"Can you go over to the side of the stage, then pretend you are coming out at the beginning of a performance. I am the first violin. The conductor always comes out with the soloist. Go ahead now."

Cathy strode off the stage, turned and came back. She took Mr. Powell's hand and shook it.

"Not bad. But not perfect," Mr. Powell said. "First of all, you are the soloist. You are the star here. The first violin knows this. Yet, because you came out this way, from the right, the audience will see my hand on top of yours." He took Cathy's hand again. "This is called having the upper hand, and because you do not have it, the audience is not with you. They have come to see a *performance*. The first violin is here all the time. Right?"

"Okay," Cathy said. "So what should I do?"

"You must demand to come from the left side of the stage." When Cathy returned, this time from the left, we all saw that it was her hand on top now. I had never thought about this before, but she did, in some ways, seem more in command.

"A little bow, Cathy," Mr. Powell said. "You don't want to seem as though you're above it all."

Cathy bowed slightly.

"The audience has now ceased their celebrations in regards to your appearance before them. They are waiting for you to perform."

I could see that Cathy believed this. She was dying to have people waiting for her to perform.

Mr. Powell pointed to her. "This is poise, people. Poise is how you present yourself. In control. Calm. Ready. If you have poise, you may then have presence. If you have presence, you will have your audience. You will have control of the stage. You will give a performance. Thank you, Cathy."

Cathy sat back down with her group. She gave a little laugh when someone said something to her. She glanced in my direction, looking very pleased with herself.

"Performance is not just what you play and how you play it," Mr. Powell said. "You must have a presence, a command of yourself and your audience. This is very important in auditions as well.

The judges are looking for someone who *commands* their attention. Not just with their playing, but with their whole being.

"Poise, presence, performance. I cannot stress these elements enough. If you are not confident, you will not look confident, and people will not hear what you are playing. Not *really* hear it. Do you understand?"

There was some conversation, but mostly we all just stared at him. I doubt many people in the room had ever considered what it meant to hold the attention of an audience. I know I hadn't.

"Okay then, practice. Set up a chair for the first violin. Someone be the conductor. Take turns. Feel what it is like to come out there with poise."

Olivia went first. She seemed fine. She bowed well, had a firm handshake. Jon jokingly tripped, tried to give me a high five, then sat on Dani's lap.

None of us laughed.

When it was my turn, I felt mostly fine. But then, as I stood before the mock audience, I became nervous again. I could feel my heart rate picking up. My hands got clammy.

It was ridiculous.

It wasn't even real—but all I could think was, Everyone is looking right at you.

"You did fine," Dani said.

But I didn't believe her. Even in this pretend situation I was losing it.

How was I going to perform for the Juilliard people?

"You're going to be great. Don't worry," Dani said.

Don't worry, they say. It'll be fine, they say.

Just do it, they say.

* * *

That afternoon I recorded a professional audition tape. I did the Paganini and a Mozart. The Mozart took two takes, the Paganini only one. I didn't feel any of the anxiety, likely because I was standing alone in a sound booth.

Mr. Powell was in the recording studio when I came out. He shook my hand, holding it between both of his. "That was remarkable. Everything was perfect on this end. Did you like it?"

"I guess."

"He guesses," Mr. Powell said to the engineer. "Play that back for him."

The engineer hit a few buttons and the sound of my violin filled the room. I heard a couple of spots where the tone wasn't quite right. Once I even nicked the D string by mistake. But it wasn't enough to redo.

"Perfect," Mr. Powell said. "Will, if you can perform like this for the Juilliard people, the world will be your oyster. Do you understand that?"

"I guess. Sure."

"You need to know." He made a fist and gave me a light bump in the chest. "You need to believe."

*   *   *

Mr. Jorgensen was waiting for me on the porch when I got home.

He was not all smiles.

"Why didn't you tell me?" he said.

"What?"

"The problems," he said. He began coughing. "Don't play dumb. Alisha has been here. She told me about your..." He waved his hand around. "Issues."

"I don't..."

"I should have made you perform, I guess," he said. "Put you in those little festivals. But no, that would have been useless. That would have been worse. People would have pulled you away. They would have told you how great you are and danced you out like their pet monkey."

I sat on the railing. The evening buses were lined up outside the apartment. I scanned the street, trying to locate an accident or construction area to explain the traffic snarl.

"You get nervous," he said.

I looked at the ground. "Yes."

"Why are you looking down? This isn't something to be ashamed about. My god, everyone gets nervous, and usually for dumber reasons than pouring their heart out in front of strangers."

"Why?" I said. "Where does it even come from?"

"I have no idea! It doesn't make sense. It's just something that happens. But it's all inside. I was nervous as anything around Alisha's mother when we first met. I couldn't eat. I could barely sleep."

"That's girls."

"It's not just girls, Will. Every time I got on the stage to conduct, I felt as though I was going to show the audience my dinner. But I never did."

How, I wanted to ask. *What was it that saved you? How did you control yourself?* But instead I said, "I'll be okay." And I figured I would be. While I was away from the stage, I couldn't even imagine the nerves I'd been feeling. It seemed stupid to me that I couldn't just get up there and do it. I could even convince myself that I would. That the next time it would be no big deal. That how I was feeling at this moment was how I'd always feel. That I was fine. Brave, strong, ready to perform.

"Everyone has to deal with this in his or her own way," he said. "It's not something I can teach you. You have to find your reason. It has to come from inside. That's the only way to defeat these nerves. This anxiety. You have to find control. Do you understand?"

Sometimes, Mr. Jorgensen could sound angry. I knew he never was, but it sometimes sounded that way. This was one of those times.

"I'll be okay," I said.

"You will," he said. "You're stronger than this."

Ten

I was excited to return to the school on Monday. It seemed as though everything would be new. The nerves would be gone. I'd be fine.

We practiced for half an hour Monday morning, then took a break.

We'd nailed the Fugue. The Adagio remained unforgiving for Olivia and Jon—although, since Jon had brought me in on his little secret, I wondered if his ineptness was a ploy to make Olivia feel better about herself. After all, if he stumbled, it wouldn't just be her screwing up.

"We can perform this no problem this afternoon," Jon said. "Piece of cake." He was staring at Olivia, who had just messed up again.

Whenever Olivia slipped up, Jon made a racket with his cello and put it aside, wiped fake sweat from his head and talked about how it was challenging or tricky.

After an hour of practice, everything had become a little too "tricky."

Dani did fine with the second-violin part. I could sense her watching me. And though the cello is the driving force in the Adagio, it felt as though the rest of the group was looking to me for guidance. Waiting for my next move before committing to an action.

It was amazing playing the lead. I felt in control. The other parts swam around mine, and if I happened to play too loudly or with more energy than necessary, it was because I was enjoying it more than I thought I would.

"I need a break," Olivia said, setting her viola down in its case.

"Me too," Jon said, and even though Olivia went straight to her phone, he followed her out of the room, talking at her. I could tell he had some kind of plan for the day. A few points of interest he wanted to bring up. He'd probably researched some of the things he'd discovered Olivia liked and was waiting to innocently drop them into conversation. Hoping to catch her interest enough for her to put the phone down for a moment and talk to him.

"He totally likes her," Dani said.

"Yeah," I replied, feeling that I wasn't giving away any of his secrets because I hadn't brought it up.

"You think so too?" Dani said.

"Now that you mention it, yeah," I said.

"I miss my boyfriend," she said, either because it was true or because she didn't want to give me the wrong idea.

"Where is he?"

"Montreal. Well, outside of Montreal, but still close. We've been together for eight months."

"Does he play anything?"

"Music? No. Soccer, yes. It's all he does. In fact, with the start of the summer season I doubt he's even noticed I'm gone."

"I'm sure he's noticed."

She'd stood and was looking out the window. "I'm just kidding," she said. "We Skype every night."

"It must suck to be away from him."

"It's only a couple of weeks, right?"

"I guess."

"And anyway, I'm going to university in the fall, and he still doesn't know what he wants to do. He says he's going to follow me to Western, but I kind of don't want that."

"Okay," I said. "Why?"

"Because it's university, you know? I don't exactly want to go out and be crazy or anything. But I need to experience everything I can." She turned to me and scrunched her face. "We talked about getting an apartment together, but I just signed up for a room in the residence. So he can come visit and stuff, but the rooms are all for two people, so he won't be able to stay the night."

I decided not to say anything. It felt like she was mostly talking to herself anyway. Getting all the thoughts out to see how they looked in the light.

"I think being together eight months is too short a time anyway. Don't you?"

"Too short for what?" I said.

"For us to move in together, I guess. For him to even come and stay the night and...for us."

"I don't know," I said.

She smiled at me. "Do you have a girlfriend?"

I almost laughed. "No."

"You want one?"

"I haven't really thought about it." Which sounded crazy but was totally the truth. It wasn't like I didn't think about girls. It was just that I hadn't ever noticed a specific girl and thought I would like to date her. Just like I had never thought about performing in front of people.

"Okay," Dani said. "That's kind of weird."

"I know."

"I don't mean that you're weird. Just that guys your age are normally girl crazy. Like we're this new thing in the world that they never noticed before and then they suddenly do and it's all they talk or think about." She crossed the room and sat next to me.

"I like girls," I said. "Just no one specific."

Danielle put her hands on my knees. "Would you like to go on a pretend date with me?"

"What?" I said.

She sighed and looked at her feet. "I've only ever dated my boyfriend. His name's Pierre, by the way, so I can stop calling him just 'my boyfriend.' Anyway, I've only ever dated him. And we've never really *dated*. Like, we go to the movies and stuff, but it's always with a group, and then when we're alone, well...I mean..." She blushed, shook her head quickly and waved a hand in front of her. "Anyway, it'd be fun for you to show me the city. Just the two of us, though, and we could pretend we were on a kind of date." She nudged me with her elbow. "Does that sound totally weird?"

"No," I lied. "I get it."

"So, you want to do that? We can go Wednesday, before this is all over. You can show me the cool things in the city, and I'll buy you dinner."

"You don't have to do that."

Olivia and Jon came back into the room. Jon was talking while Olivia tapped away on her phone.

"I asked you out," Dani whispered. "So I pay for dinner. That's how it works. Even if it is just pretend."

I leaned into her. She smelled like tangerines. "Okay," I said. "Sounds fun."

Eleven

"Why aren't the Juilliard people going to be here?" Olivia whined.

It was Wednesday, the third to last day of the workshop. I had spent the morning working on solo pieces. We'd all had lunch together, but otherwise it was a time to perfect our pieces alone.

Mr. Powell held his hands out. "They're caught up with something else," he said. "I am sorry."

Olivia seemed on the verge of tears. "Is there no way we can perform later? Maybe they'll show up eventually."

"The representatives have said they can't be here at all today," he said. "Which is why we'll be doing the solo performances tomorrow. But there simply isn't enough time to do both the group and solo concerts at the same time."

After Mr. Powell left, Olivia turned to the rest of us. "Why should we even bother?"

"He said we can just do the Fugue if we want," Jon said. "That's good."

"For those people?" Olivia said, pointing at the other students. "I mean, honestly, who cares?"

"It's a performance," Jon said. "It shouldn't matter who is listening. Let's just go out and kill it."

"We've practiced really hard," Dani said.

It seemed to me Olivia did care but was completely deflated.

"I can't come back here next year," she said. "I'll be nineteen."

"Are you going to university for music?"

"Yeah, but just..." She sighed. "I really wanted to go to Juilliard. Not for undergrad, but once I graduate. I want to be in New York. I need out of here."

"Mr. Powell said they'd record all the performances," Jon said. "So that should work. You can still get your performance to the Juilliard people."

"It's not the same," Olivia said.

I understood what she meant. It isn't the same. As Mr. Powell said, a recording lacks poise and presence. At first, I was happy to not even think about going out onstage. I was almost ready to go along with Olivia and say forget it. But we had worked hard, and I could tell Dani really wanted to do the performance. It meant something to her, though I didn't know what.

"Let's do this," I said.

"Really? Hulk-Aid, are you sure?"

"That has not caught on," Dani said.

"Yes, I mean it," I said.

"No freak-outs?"

"None." I didn't feel nervous. Well, not passing-out, falling-down, it's-the-end-of-the-world-as-we-know-it nervous. I felt my nerves. The anxiety there. But I was with these other three people. We were going to perform together.

"Fine," Olivia said. "But I'm not going to like it."

*　*　*

There was no great spectacle getting on the stage. We walked out, our instruments ready, sat in the chairs, turned to the first page of the Fugue and waited for everyone to be quiet.

It took a while.

I waited for the voice of doubt to creep in. But as I did, I watched Danielle. She inhaled deeply, then let the air out in a slow, steady stream. Almost two whole weeks of practices and lectures, workshops and group classes, for this.

I was doing it for her.

No one cared that we were on the stage. Well, maybe some of them did, but not enough to stop chatting.

Mr. Powell clapped his hands, and everyone came to attention.

"Hey, everyone, we're DJ OW!" Jon said. "Check out this crazy tune."

"Oh my god, what a loser."

It was Cathy, standing directly in front of us. She brought her phone out and held it up in front of her. "Put on a good show, Will."

"What are you doing?" Olivia whispered at Jon.

"Softening up the crowd," Jon said. "Ready?"

I looked away from Cathy. Then I heard a little beep as she began recording on her phone.

We readied our instruments and played.

My head did not explode.

My insides did not fall out.

I didn't pass out, drop my bow or in any way mess up. I just played. The whole time, I kept an eye on Danielle. Watching her as she enjoyed every second of it. How she lived in the moment.

Once, while I had a quick break in the piece, I looked at Mr. Powell, who was standing with Alisha. He had his eyes closed, his lips closed tight. Alisha was smiling as though she was pulling the music into her.

I glanced at Cathy; she scowled back. I considered giving her a wink, but I wasn't that brave. And soon enough it was over.

"That kicked ass," Jon said as we were putting our instruments away. The next group had already taken to the stage.

"It really worked," Danielle said.

Jon punched me on the shoulder.

"And no Hulk-Aid," he said. "How'd you do it?"

I didn't tell him how I'd thought of Mr. Jorgensen being nervous every time he stepped on the stage. Or how I'd pretended we were in our practice room alone. I didn't even tell him how I'd practiced the piece so many times that I likely could have been half comatose and still pulled it off.

And I didn't tell him it was because I was playing for Danielle.

"It's fun playing with you guys," I said. "I guess that's all."

"Fun." Jon shrugged. "Okay, whatever floats your boat."

When we had our instruments put away, Danielle leaned over and whispered in my ear. "It's time for our date."

"What about the other performances?"

"I don't think we'll be missed. Come on, I need to get out of here."

I looked to the stage. Cathy was there, glaring at one of her group members.

"Okay," I said, as Cathy began to berate the cellist. "Let's go."

Twelve

t first I thought the sound of the violin was in my head. Then I noticed a girl standing on the corner of York and William Streets. I'd seen buskers in the ByWard Market before, but usually a guy with a beat-up guitar or one of those people who dress all in silver and only move, like, once an hour.

The girl with the violin was maybe eighteen or nineteen. She was good. The market was filled with music that night, yet people stopped to listen to her, dropping coins into her open case before going on their way. Beside us, through an open window in the Château Lafayette, we saw a TV showing a baseball game, men with fingers wrapped around bottles staring intensely at the screen. Someone bumped me as they passed, and Dani pulled me to the wall of a parking garage.

"She's good," Dani said.

"Yeah," I replied. I was nodding my head to the music.

Occasionally the girl dipped her head toward the ground and added a little flourish to her bowing.

At first I thought she was showing off. But soon I saw that she was completely entranced by the music. She'd fallen into what she was playing. Coaxing each note out of her instrument. There were mistakes, of course, and the sound was a bit flat—though that could have been the violin itself. But for this crowd, these people wandering through the market on a hazy summer evening, she was playing something completely beautiful.

When she finished the piece, the small crowd that had gathered around her clapped. More money dropped into her case. Children ran up and thanked her.

Danielle and I walked through the market. I pointed out the places I knew. The statues and buskers. The restaurants I'd eaten in. I showed her where a great bookstore once stood. Most of the market area was now full of pubs and expensive restaurants.

"That was awesome," Dani said out of nowhere. She grabbed my hand. We were standing in front of a store that seemed to sell only soap.

"What?" I said.

"Our performance. It was awesome. We totally nailed it."

"It was great," I said.

She squeezed my hand. "Thank you," she said. Then she let go and pointed at a nearby store. "We need to go in there."

"Why?"

"Because we totally rocked that concert and I want to celebrate with new shoes."

I had never been in Top of the World—or in any of the trendy stores—and was amazed by all the shirts and skateboards and the sheer number of different decks and wheels available. It was like a different world. When Mr. Jorgensen and I came into the market, we always went to the same independent coffee shop. Sometimes he stopped in at the bike shop where his nephew worked, and other times we wandered up to the National Gallery.

Dani bought a pair of deep-blue etnies and a fat leather bracelet. As we were leaving the store, she wrapped the bracelet around my wrist.

It seemed strange there—I'd never worn any jewelry. "What's this for?" I asked.

"For remembering me," she said.

I wanted to tell her I wouldn't forget her, but the words didn't come out.

"Is this place good?" Dani asked. We'd worked our way back around to William Street, and ended up outside a restaurant named Vittoria Trattoria, where the violinist was busking.

"I have no idea."

"Let's try it."

We went inside and were given a window seat.

Before taking our order, the waiter brought out a little basket of bread. We were both starved and grabbed pieces—but there was one hard little bun we both avoided.

Eventually, Dani picked it up. "What's with this guy?" she said, knocking it on the table.

I took it and knocked it on the window, then set it in the middle of the table. "Is it supposed to be like this?"

Dani grabbed it from me. "Maybe."

"Who would eat that?"

She looked at me, tilting her head to one side. "Truth or eat the bun," she said.

"What?" I said.

"Truth or eat the bun," she said again. "We'll ask each other a question and whoever doesn't answer their question has to eat this bun. And you have to be totally honest. If you're not totally honest and the other person calls you out, you have to eat the bun."

"Okay," I said. "Like, the whole bun?"

"Yes, all of it. Who knows though—it could be really good."

"I doubt that."

"Same here," she said. "You start."

"How?" I said.

"Ask me a question. Anything. I'll answer it honestly."

"Do you love your boyfriend?"

She sat back in her seat, thinking. I didn't even know why I'd asked that. It just seemed to be something she was struggling with. Something I could force her to be honest about, for better or worse.

"Right out of the gates, eh?" She took a sip of water and opened her eyes wide. "I don't know."

"Eat the bun."

"No. That's the honest truth. I've told him I love him. He said it back. So that was all taken care of. But right after I said it, I wasn't sure if I believed it. I'm still not."

"Okay," I said. "You don't have to eat the bun."

She banged it on the table. "That makes me ridiculously happy."

"Your go."

"If you could be anything, what would you be?"

"Like, now? Or when I grow up?" I asked.

She laughed.

"What?"

"When you 'grow up.' That just sounds dumb."

"Sorry," I said.

"Don't be sorry. It's just that I'm about to go to university, and we're supposed to feel all grown up and act differently and everything. But yeah, you're fifteen. So...when you grow up."

"A violinist," I said.

"Honestly?"

"Absolutely. A soloist as well. Like James Ehnes." As I said this, I realized it was true. But at the same time, the idea felt fresh and new.

Our dinners came. I'd ordered a plain-sounding pizza. Danielle had seafood lasagna. The table immediately smelled like the ocean.

"Your go," Danielle said.

"Why did you come to the workshop?"

She scrunched up her nose. "Honestly?"

I pointed at the bun.

"Okay. Because I had to prove to myself that I was good enough. Getting in was hard. Okay, actually—so I don't have to eat that bun—I'm here because I had to prove to everyone else that I was good enough. And by everyone else I mean my friends and Pierre. Mostly just so they'll leave me alone. You should have seen people when I told them I was coming. They were all, like, amazed that I had made it in. As though what I'm doing is some stupid hobby. So who cares? Because it's classical music."

She paused and took another drink of water. "That's why I'm here, I guess. For them. Because when I told them about this program and how hard it was to get in, there was this little bit of recognition that maybe, just maybe, all the practice I did and everything else actually mattered. That it was as important as when Pierre scored a goal. Only when I get a piece down, there's no applause. Right? But no one has *any* idea about these things. I mean, what *is* success in classical music?"

"What is success in anything?"

"People are famous for being famous these days. So, honestly, what does talent matter?"

"I think it does," I said. "I mean, I think it's important."

"So do I. But that doesn't make it a lot easier. Anyway, I'm going to university for business. It's what my parents have always wanted and, in a way, what I want as well."

"Not music?"

"No. I mean, I know how good I am. I don't have a career in music waiting for me."

"Will you keep playing?"

She shrugged again. "Who knows? That concert we just put on kind of felt like the end for me. A final thing so I can tell myself I did it, that I tried."

"But you could teach or be in music some other way."

"I might be able to do something, sure. Anything is possible, right?" She grabbed the bun and banged it on the table. "You're hogging all the questions. It's my turn." She shook the bun at me. "Why do you get so nervous?"

I almost denied it. Instead, I set my fork down and looked at her. "Because I don't want to fail," I said. Which felt honest.

"You won't. Why else?"

"Because I don't want to make a fool of myself."

"Not going to happen. You're annoyingly amazing. Why else?" I didn't say anything, so she bumped my nose with the bun. "Taste the bun. Feel its ridiculous staleness. Imagine biting the bun." She bumped my nose again. "Why do you really get so nervous?"

"Because..." I looked at my pizza. Listened to the girl playing violin. Thought about what Jon had said. What Mr. Jorgensen had talked about. I even considered all the things I'd read on the Internet, and still I came up blank.

But the answer was there. I just didn't want to admit it.

"Okay, eat the bun," Danielle said.

"I don't want to eat the bun," I said.

"Then be honest. Why do you get so nervous?"

"Because it matters," I finally said.

And it felt as if a weight had slid from my shoulders. The waiter was standing beside our table, asking if he could take anything away. Danielle looked at me.

I said it again. "Because it matters."

She put the bun in the basket and handed it to the waiter.

"Of course it does," she said.

*   *   *

We'd finished dinner, having discussed everything from *Teenage Mutant Ninja Turtles* to the differences between *Back to the Future I, II* and *III*, and were outside walking when Dani said, "That's the way you have to think about it."

"About what?" I said. We'd just been talking about the best strategy in a zombie apocalypse.

"Your nerves. Your worrying about it mattering. You have to ask yourself, Who does it matter to?"

"Me," I said. "Before this, I'd assumed I'd always be playing violin. I'd never thought about the future. And now that I know I want to do this forever, it matters. It's like all these people are suddenly involved in my life. They get to decide where I go. What I can do. It's painful."

"That's because you're thinking of it the wrong way. One mistake isn't going to end your life."

"Are you sure?" I said.

She stopped and turned to me. "Will, you are incredible. You are the best violinist I have ever heard. It seems entirely effortless for you. Honestly, you're annoying as hell."

"Thanks," I said.

"You're welcome. So here's the thing. You need to play for yourself. It's what you've been doing for years, right?"

"Sure," I said. "And for Mr. Jorgensen."

"Why did you play for him?"

I thought back to Mr. Jorgensen laughing and clapping while I played. Of the smile on his face.

Of the joy it seemed to bring him.

"Because he loves it," I said.

"So don't change anything, Will. Keep playing for yourself. And play for people who love it. Forget the judges. Forget what might or might not happen next. You need to play for yourself."

The violin girl was playing some modern piece I'd never heard before.

"Look at her," Dani said. "Look at the people listening to her. Do you think any of them care if one note is slightly off or if she forgets something halfway through?"

The crowd around the violinist seemed entranced by her playing.

"I guess not," I said.

"I *know* not. She's communicating with them. She's telling them something important and they're getting it. That's what we do as musicians. We talk to one another through our instruments. But in the end, you also have to make sure you don't take it all too seriously."

"Don't take it too seriously," I repeated.

"Nothing is ever the end of the world," she added.

"Except the zombie apocalypse," I said.

"Yeah." She shuddered. "That would be awful."

Thirteen

The following day, we had individual practice in the morning. Mr. Powell came into the small practice room and listened as I played my piece. It was seriously uncomfortable. There isn't really enough room for two people in those rooms, and his cologne filled the space completely.

"Will, that is remarkable," he said. He opened the door and stepped out. People were walking along the corridor, and the sound of failure hung in the air. Failure in the best way. A missed note followed by a slice of silence, then another try. Try after try after try: this is how music is made.

"Thank you." I stuck my head out the door and inhaled.

"I would like you to perform first tomorrow. Would that be okay with you?"

"Yes." After talking with Dani the night before, I'd tried to change the way I looked at performing. I got nervous because it mattered. It mattered because music was such a central part of me. I was putting my whole self out there.

"Fantastic. And we'll see you at the concert this evening?"

"Absolutely," I said. James Ehnes was performing at Chamberfest that night. But first he would be visiting the workshop to talk to us. If I was nervous about anything, it was being in the same room as James Ehnes.

* * *

Things were a little strange at lunch. I hadn't seen Dani all morning, and though it was totally normal to sit with her, now it felt different somehow. She patted my knee, asked how I was feeling.

"Great," I said.

"How'd your practice go this morning?"

"Great."

"You excited about seeing James Ehnes?"

"It'll be great."

"Have you lost most of your vocabulary?"

"What?"

"You're answering everything in one-word sentences."

"Sorry," I said. She opened her eyes wide at me. "Everything's fine. Really."

"That's better. It was a lot of fun last night."

"It was," I said.

Olivia and Jon were suddenly standing above us. I didn't immediately recognize Olivia, as her cell phone was in a pocket somewhere. It was strange to see her full face.

"This egg salad is awful," Jon said, sitting down. "Why do I keep eating it?"

"You feel the need to punish yourself," Olivia said, sliding in beside him.

"I must." Jon stared at the sandwich. "I think there's shell in this one. At least, I hope that's shell."

"What are we doing this afternoon?" Olivia asked.

"James Ehnes is coming in to talk to us. Then we're all going to the concert," Dani said.

"Do we have to dress up for this thing?" Jon said.

Olivia raised her chin toward him. "What, do you always want to wear those shorts and that T-shirt?"

"This is my look," Jon said.

"Consider an upgrade," Olivia said, leaving Jon to examine his clothes and then wrap the egg sandwich in a napkin and shoot it deftly into a nearby garbage can.

A shadow fell over us.

"You guys did all right yesterday." Cathy was above us, her cell in hand. She turned the phone around. She'd recorded the whole performance, it seemed. "You slowed up here, though, and then, for no reason at all, sped way up." She turned the phone back toward herself. "It seems as though Will was your leader." She looked at me. "Do you have tempo issues?"

"It was good," Dani said. "We were really good."

"I mean, if you're as special as everyone says, then tempo should be, like, simple."

"Hey, Cathy?" I said.

"Yes, Special?"

"Shut up." It felt good letting that out. "Seriously."

"Rude much?" she said.

Dani was laughing behind her hand.

"What?" Cathy said to her.

"Just what he said," Dani said. "Seriously, shut up. We're all tired of hearing from you."

"You might have noticed that during *my* performance—"

"We wouldn't have noticed," Dani interrupted. "Because we left."

"What? Everyone was supposed to stay for the recital."

"What can you do?" Dani said. "We had other business."

"Well, Alisha needs to know about this."

"She probably does," Dani said. "Why don't you run off and tell her now."

Cathy narrowed her eyes and pursed her lips. She seemed on the verge of saying something else, but instead turned and walked away.

"That was awesome," Jon said.

"Do you think she'll ever talk to us again?" Olivia said.

"Hopefully not," I said.

"All right, everyone." Alisha was at the double doors leading to the lecture hall. "James is here to talk to us."

* * *

I'll admit I was starstruck.

We came into the room and James Ehnes was standing off to one side of the stage with his accompanist, Andrew Armstrong. They were both smiling and nodding to people as we sat down. There was a quiet in the room different than we'd experienced in the whole two weeks. It was as though their presence had frozen the crowd.

Then Andrew Armstrong said, "I feel as though a Requiem should be playing." There were a few laughs, and then the voices rose again to a roar.

"Everyone, quickly, find a seat," Alisha said. All talk quieted. "We are so pleased to welcome multi-award-winning violinist James Ehnes to our little workshop." She opened her mouth to say more, then stopped, and everyone laughed. " I want to go on about James, but I think it's better to just hear from the man himself. Students, James Ehnes."

James walked to the center of the stage in an eruption of applause. He smiled and nodded at us. He was in a light shirt and jeans, which was amazing to me. I'd always thought of him as someone who wore a suit all the time. Which is dumb, I know, but it was the only way I'd ever seen him.

"It is great to see all of you here," he said. "It takes me back to my time at Meadowmount. The excitement of playing every day. Of working with professionals and just being in the same room as all these other people who love the same thing you do. I don't have a real talk arranged, so if you'd like to ask some questions, I'd be happy to answer them."

Hands went up. People asked about Juilliard (amazing, influential). About how much his violin was worth (lots). About whom he enjoyed performing with the most (he said Andrew, but then they both laughed, so who knows). Where, when, what. It was endless, and he answered all the questions with a calmness and ease I found amazing.

So I put my hand up.

"Yes?"

"Do you ever get nervous?"

He nodded and looked right at me.

"I do. I did. I will," he said. "If you don't feel an energy before you go onstage, then something is missing. But are those nerves? I don't know. I don't think so." James shrugged and moved to the other side of the stage.

He didn't seem nervous to me. Not at all.

"I like to think that the energy is anticipation," he said. "The desire to perform. To give a crowd of people music. I can't imagine any better feeling. I am a vehicle for the music, which might sound New Agey or whatever, but it's true. It's why I learned to play. Why I keep learning. Why I never stop practicing and performing. I love classical music, and I want to bring it to people. I always think, There must be dozens of people out there who have never heard this piece before. I want them to love it as much as I do. I need to play with everything I have inside of me to express the music."

He stopped and looked at me again. "So yes, there is energy, but not really nerves. If you get nervous, think of it differently. Think of it as your body preparing to exhaust itself with the effort. But most of all, we need to get used to things."

He smiled. "And the only way to get used to anything is to do whatever it is again and again. So in order to be less nervous about performing, you need to perform more. It takes a lot of courage to get up there that first time, the second time, the twenty-fifth time, but eventually, it is just something you do. Does that help?"

"Yes," I said.

"Good." James turned to Andrew Armstrong. "Anything to add, Andy?"

"When you're as good-looking as I am, you just worry whether people will hear the music at all." There was a lot of laughter. "I mean, seriously, who can pay attention to the performance?"

"Right. Any other questions?" James said.

There were more. Many more. After a while Alisha took to the stage and thanked James, letting him know we'd all be at the concert that night. James thanked us and bowed before he and Andrew left.

"I think we could all use a break before the concert tonight," Alisha said. "We'll see you at Chamberfest. Please consider what you wear. I know it'll be hot tonight, but let's try and have some decency."

"Decency," Jon said, looking at his Scooby-Doo T-shirt and wrinkled shorts. "I'm totally decent."

* * *

The four of us decided to meet outside the church where the concert was going to happen. Jon was in a pair of black trousers, with a green jacket and blue tie. I'd have said it was a bad idea, but somehow it worked. Olivia was wearing a dress. She took a picture of Jon with her cell phone, then hunched over it as we waited in line.

We were almost inside by the time Dani arrived.

"Sorry," she said as she slipped into the line beside me. "Just talking to Pierre."

"Oh," I said. "How'd that go?"

She shrugged. "I told him I've decided to live on campus next year."

"Oh," I said again. "And?"

"Yeah. Well." She smiled. "We should go in."

The church was hot and muggy. Fans blew air around the large room but not enough to make it comfortable. We found space on a pew and crammed in behind Mr. Powell and Alisha.

"Are you excited?" Alisha asked us.

"Absolutely," Jon said. He was smushed against Olivia, so I wasn't certain whether he was excited about that or the performance.

Olivia held her phone out in front of us and took what Jon explained would be an "epic group selfie" but which ended up showing us with seriously extended chins and half-closed eyes. She was about to try again when someone shut off all the fans and dimmed the lights.

Andrew and James came out together and bowed. As Andrew settled behind the piano, James introduced the piece. "Tonight we will be performing Sonata in D Major, Op. 9, No. 3, by Jean-Marie Leclair."

"Oh," Andrew said. He pulled the sheet music in front of him off the piano and replaced it with another. This got a good laugh.

"You ready back there?" James asked.

Andrew nodded. "Absolutely."

And with that, they began.

It was incredible. What James had said about delivering the music was totally correct. It just rolled out of him. It seemed effortless, but I knew there was practice behind it. Hours and days and weeks and years of practice. He looked entirely at peace on the stage. As though he could be playing in his living room or busking on a street corner. He kept his eyes trained on his violin, his head snapping to the speed of the music now and then. His fingers moved so sleekly that it seemed they were everywhere at once.

I'd seen him play before, but this time I was in the second row. I heard the thud of Andrew hitting the pedal on the piano a couple of times. I didn't know the piece, but it didn't seem as though either of them made any mistakes. I closed my eyes and tried to hold the music in me. Tried to let it flow through my body like something that had gotten into my bloodstream.

Three encores later, they finally left the stage.

And I felt like a new person.

Fourteen

"I'm going to play," I said to myself, bending down to bring my violin out of its case.

My mind was already leaning toward total failure. "I am playing for myself. I am playing because I love it. I am playing because it's what I do," I whispered. I tried to recall James the night before. The calmness that he had brought with him to the stage. The poise.

My head was dizzy, my hands sweaty. I could have given in at that moment. I could have simply put down my violin and stopped. Walked away. Quit for good. But I wanted to play. That was the thing. I *wanted* to play this piece. Not *for* anyone, but just to play it. To hear it fill that room. To watch the notes wash over everyone.

"Paganini," I said. "Caprice No. 24 in A Minor."
I caught a smile from James Ehnes. We'd done a master class with him that morning. In the end, there were only three of us admitted: Elliott, Sung and I. James had seemed really impressed with my playing but still had a lot of suggestions for how I could make it better. A shift of the wrist, a different angle on the D string. Little things I'd never even thought of.

The hall was full of people. I looked up, set my violin in place, inhaled deeply and played.

It was like every other time I'd played the piece. A flurry of motion. A mess of notes all dancing around in front of me, just waiting for me to catch up. I didn't notice what the audience was doing. Not even James Ehnes. I just watched those notes moving along in front of me and plucked them out, one by one. It was like running really quickly without letting up. Like swimming through some glassy lake.

And soon enough, it was over.

People were clapping.

My hands were still sweaty, my heart was pounding, my legs felt slightly wobbly, but I was done.

Someone shouted "Bravo!" I looked to see Andrew Armstrong clapping and nudging James in the arm. "Bravo!" he yelled again.

I didn't fall down the stairs getting off the stage either, which had been my irrational fear the second I finished playing. I just tucked my violin under one arm and walked off.

It hadn't been easy, getting up there. Holding that bow. Clearing my mind. None of it was easy. But I did it.

"Well, you blew them away," Danielle said as I put my violin into its case. "One of the guys from Juilliard kept shaking his head. Like, in disbelief."

"Can I have your autograph?" Jon said.

"No," I said. "You're not worthy."

"Ohhhh, snap," he said. He was still laughing when Alisha came over with James Ehnes.

James Ehnes put his hand out.

James Ehnes smiled.

James Ehnes said, "That was very impressive."

James Ehnes took my hand and shook it. Then he put his hands in his pockets and said, "I played that on my first CD."

"I know," I managed.

"It's a thrilling piece. The dynamics are so intricate."

"Yes," I said.

James Ehnes smiled at me again. "You have a bright future ahead," he said. "Enjoy every second of it." Then someone called his name and he was ushered away by a woman with sleek brown hair and stunning blue eyes.

"That was exceptional, Will," Alisha said.

"Thank you," I said.

"You seemed fine up there. Were you fine?"

"I was fine," I said. "It was good."

"It *was* good," she said. Then she grabbed my head in both her hands and kissed my forehead. "It was triumphant."

I didn't feel triumphant or perfect or successful or any of the other things people told me I was. I'd played the piece the way I wanted to. For a brief moment, just the length of that piece, I had silenced the fear. I'd pushed it out of me altogether, right down into the stage and beyond, farther, deeper. I'd buried it underground.

But I knew it would always be there.

* * *

There was a closing reception that night.

I danced with Danielle to a horrible pop song. It made no sense to me that the school had hired some hack DJ for this party. Then again, it wasn't like we loved only classical music. We could dance. We could laugh at the ridiculous lyrics and at times sing along.

Somehow Jon got to the DJ, and before the night was over at least four Swedish hip-hop songs had been played.

Danielle and I drank punch and watched Jon dancing with Olivia. I can't say I have ever seen anyone look happier. First it was a fast dance, where they kind of shuffled around one another. Then a slow one. She even leaned her head against his shoulder once.

I wondered which touchstone had worked for Jon. What connection he'd managed to make. Or maybe Olivia had seen what real people had to offer over virtual ones.

The party went on deep into the night, but since I wasn't staying at the university, I said my goodbyes, accepted the congratulations from everyone and got on a bus for home.

I could mostly see just my reflection in the window of the bus. Bits of the outside world hovered to the surface now and then, only to disappear again. A bunch of university kids got on at one stop, drunk and talking too loudly about things I couldn't even understand. Punching each other in a jovial way I'd never made sense of. Bothering everyone else on the bus. I kept to my seat, hunkered down.

For the past two weeks I'd felt more myself than I ever had at school—or even with my friends. Everyone at the workshop was, in some way, like me. If nothing else, we had music to bring us together. A common understanding of how playing one note after another made us feel.

Kept us alive.

Fifteen

Under a gray, dim sky, I returned to the university in the morning.

Alisha was the first person I saw. She was coming out of the administration building, looking not unlike my mother after a day in a government office.

"Will," she said. "What are you doing here?"

"I just came to say goodbye to everyone."

"Of course, yes. They'll be packing up in the dorm." She sat on a bench. "What a great two weeks."

"For sure," I said, sitting next to her.

"And I understand you're going to New York to audition at Juilliard?"

"I am," I said.

"You'll do great, Will," Alisha said.

The call had come in the night before. Mr. Cain, one of the administrative people who had been at the concert, had phoned before I'd even gotten home. My father had told him we'd be there, even though they wanted me to audition the very next week.

"I'm pretty lucky to have the kind of parents who will drop everything and take me to New York."

"You are. Juilliard is paying for the trip as well, I hear?"

"Yeah."

"They really want you there, Will. They see your talent. They see the type of musician you could become. It's so exciting." She squeezed my hand and shook it.

"Thank you," I said. "For everything."

"I did nothing. It was my father." Her eyes turned to the sky. "He hasn't been well. Have you noticed?"

"A little."

"He's going in for more tests today. I'm taking him this afternoon. It might be nothing, but you never know."

"I'll see him tomorrow," I said.

"Hopefully." She let go of my hand and patted my knees. "You take care of yourself. Practice for the audition. Get excited about this, Will. It's the greatest opportunity you can imagine."

I saw Jon coming out of the dorm and stood up. I didn't want him to leave before I said goodbye. "I have to run," I said to Alisha.

"Of course. Come by tomorrow if you can. I'm sure Dad will be fine."

I darted across the road to the dorm just as a car pulled up. "Jon!" I yelled. I stumbled on the curb and kind of scrambled toward him.

"Hulk-Aid, slow down."

The trunk of the car opened. I could see a man in the driver's seat—Jon's dad, I assumed—talking on his cell phone.

"So, you're leaving?" I asked Jon.

"Um, yeah, it's over."

I nodded a million times, then picked up one of his bags. "And...Olivia?"

"We're going to facebook. But honestly, she's an older woman. I don't stand that much of a chance."

"You tried," I said.

"Tried? I guess you didn't notice us totally making out on the dance floor last night." He winked at me.

"I didn't notice that."

"That's because it never happened," Jon said, laughing. "Take it easy, Will. I hope you get whatever it is you want."

"Same to you," I said.

I threw his bag into the trunk.

"Yeah, well, I'm going to need to figure out what that is first," he said. He put his hand out and we did an exaggerated handshake before he slipped into the car. "Dani's still up there, if you want to say goodbye. Olivia lives in Ottawa, so I think she's already gone."

"I'll go say 'bye." I gave the hood of the car a quick triple thump, then turned before I had to watch it drive away.

I settled down on a bench in front of the dorm and watched the door, hoping there wasn't some other exit Dani could leave by. I'd been there about fifteen minutes when Cathy stepped out.

When she saw me, she put down her suitcase and sniffed as though there was a bad smell in the area. "Don't you live here?" she said.

"Yeah."

"And so you just hang around at the university?"

"No, I'm just saying goodbye to some people." I waited a moment. I was about to ask her why she had to be so cruel and petty. But I already knew the answer. She saw everyone as competition. People whom she had to be better than. Maybe it was because I'd never been a part of the whole classical-music crowd in Ottawa, or anywhere else, but viewing other musicians as my competition had never crossed my mind. I couldn't see what good it would do anyone. It seemed to have left Cathy feeling bitter.

"So I guess you are special after all," she said.

"I don't think so."

"Yeah, do the humble thing. That kills people." She picked her suitcase back up and started off down the ramp.

"Hey, Cathy," I said.

"Yeah?"

"Good luck with everything." For a second, I thought she was going to respond. Instead, she carried on down the ramp without another word.

"What are you doing here?" I turned back from watching Cathy's slow descent to find Dani beside me.

"Oh, I came to say goodbye to everyone."

"Including Cathy?"

"We traded pleasantries."

"Oh, did you?"

"Something like that." I stood and took her bag from her.

"I didn't want to leave my room," she said. "but they kicked us out to clean the place."

It was just after ten in the morning. "Want to hang out?"

"Sure," she said, looping her arm in mine.

We left her luggage in the administration building, and instead of turning toward the market, we walked over the Laurier Avenue Bridge and down to the canal. Boats slowly moved along the waterway, along with a class of stand-up paddle boarders who bounced, jittered and held on for dear life against every wave.

We stopped to look up at the National Arts Centre as we passed. "You'll play in there one day," Dani said.

"I doubt that."

"I don't. Not for a minute."

"What about you?" I said. "Are you going to keep playing?"

"I don't know. Maybe. I mean, for myself. I don't have what it takes to make it."

"Sure you—"

"I don't. I might have thought I did before, but after hearing you and some of the other people these last two weeks, I know I don't. I love playing though. That's enough."

We walked along the pathway, dodging runners and cyclists. Eventually we stopped at the hot-dog stand Mr. Jorgensen and I always went to. I had just enough to buy two dogs and a bag of fries.

"Not quite up to the dinner you bought us, but..." I said.

We sat on the grass and let the sun wash over us. There was just enough of a breeze to cool us off. "So, I'm going to New York," I said. "To audition for Juilliard."

Dani punched me on the arm. "Shut up."

"Yeah."

"That is awesome. See, that's what I mean. You have it. Juilliard is not knocking down my door."

"And that's okay, right?"

"Sure. I had dreams. But dreams change. Will, I am so happy for you."

"I still have to get in," I said.

"You will." She shook her head in disbelief. "What a ride you're getting on."

"So...thanks," I said.

"For what?"

"For helping me. Like, with my nerves."

"Nerves," she said, tossing the hot-dog wrapper into a garbage can. "They can't hold you back." She punched me again and laughed. "I doubt anything can."

Sixteen

Mr. Jorgensen had a monitor hooked up to his chest and a big electric box on the table beside him when I went to visit the next day.

"I'm pretty certain they're testing to make sure I'm still alive," he said.

I laughed.

"Don't laugh—there have been doubts."

I took my regular seat.

He looked really tired. "They've also got me on some drugs that make me sleepy, so don't expect very vibrant conversation here."

"Okay," I said. "Did you hear about Juilliard?"

"Did I hear about Juilliard," he said. "Of course I did. And of course you're going. And of course they're going to let you in." He looked to the ceiling. "We'll miss you here."

"It's just an audition."

"An audition is one thing, Will, if you *apply* to a place like that. They bring in hundreds of people just to make sure the future of music doesn't slip through their fingers. But they've *asked* you to come after hearing you. This isn't an audition, Will. This is those two scouts who were here showing you off to their friends. A big 'Look what we found in sleepy old Ottawa.'"

"You think so?"

"Pack your bags, Will. You might not be coming back." He laughed. The laugh turned into a cough. "I couldn't be prouder of you."

"Thanks," I said.

"Everything that happens from here on in is entirely due to your love of the music. It's a dying art, Will. But you will keep it alive."

"No pressure," I said.

"No, Will. No pressure at all. You keep playing for yourself and let the rest of the world decide what it is you're doing."

"I'll try." A bus stopped outside and I turned to look, as I always do. A bunch of people got off.

The last three were kids with skateboards. They rolled down the street, grinding and sliding off anything they could and looking totally carefree.

"I think I'm going to get a skateboard," I said jokingly as I turned back around. I didn't get an answer, though, because Mr. Jorgensen was already asleep.

Seventeen

We arrived at the airport later than we'd intended. I'd stopped at Mr. Jorgensen's door half a dozen times that morning, but he wasn't there.

"I'm sure he's fine," my mother said. "Alisha said he's had a lot of appointments lately."

"Okay," I said. But I had a strange feeling that this time it wasn't just an appointment. That something had happened.

Something bad.

Then we were in the airport, and there were people everywhere and none of us knew where to go. My mother wanted to buy a magazine, something she never did, and my father spent ten minutes trying to understand why you had to empty out all your water, so by the time we actually got into the International Departures line, there was a good chance we were going to miss our plane entirely.

I kept looking back at the giant inner space of the airport. There were TVs everywhere, and a steadily descending waterfall covered most of one wall. People with cell phones pressed to their ears. Kids holding their parents' hands on the escalator. And so much noise. It seemed as though a new announcement blared from the speaker system every five seconds. I was so enthralled by all the motion and noise and the immensity of the place that I didn't even see him at first.

Mr. Jorgensen.

Alisha was there, pushing her father in a wheelchair. She left him a short distance away and rushed over to us. "I'm so sorry we weren't there to see you off. Dad had an incident last night when he was at my place, and we've been at the hospital."

He looked even more fragile sitting there.

"Is he okay?" I said.

"He will be," Alisha said. "As much as he can be." She said hello to my parents. The line shifted ahead of us.

"Isn't he going to come over?" I asked.

"Yes," she said. "He wants to say goodbye. They gave him some drugs this morning that are making it really difficult for him to speak. So you might not get much more than a couple of words."

"Okay." I wasn't completely sure what was going on, but I could see that Alisha was very concerned.

"He shouldn't be here, but there was no way I could keep him away."

"Can we get out of line and see him?" I asked my father.

"We're tight for time," he said. The line behind us stretched all the way into an area that was not cordoned off. It would take forever to get back to where we were now. My mom let people pass as Alisha stepped away. While she was walking back to her father, I had an idea. I quickly set my violin case on the floor and opened it. It only took a moment for me to get the instrument out and tighten my bow. As Alisha came back, pushing her father, I began to play. Silence swept through the terminal like a wave, leaving only the sound of my violin in its wake.

Or, at least, that was how it felt.

I played Bartók's Sonata for Solo Violin—Melodia (Adagio). Slow. Steady. Letting each note flow from my fingers. Letting the sound escape the violin as though it had been freed from prison. Or as though it hadn't ever existed until I thought to create it.

Mr. Jorgensen smiled. He brought a hand to his face. Pretended he wasn't wiping away a tear. As I finished, he slowly nodded to me.

Everyone around us applauded. I held my violin beneath my arm. Held my bow firmly in one hand. And bowed.

But I was only bowing for Mr. Jorgensen.

"Adagio," he said, still nodding. "At ease."

"Thank you," I said. "For everything."

The line pushed us forward. We were out of time.

"You're welcome, my boy."

"I'll see you when I get back," I said.

He smiled briefly. "Absolutely."

We pushed through the doors to the security check. The guard, a man almost exactly my height with a big beard and thick black-rimmed glasses, looked at my violin as I was attempting to get it back in its case. "Was that you playing out there?"

"It was," I said.

"That was beautiful."

"Thank you," I said.

"No, thank *you*. You just made my day."

It was as if I was gathering people's emotions. As if every time someone listened and really heard what I was playing, I was pushing the voice of doubt farther and farther down. I knew it wasn't going to be easy. That the fear would flare up again, shaking my body, clouding my mind. But I also knew I could control it.

That I just had to play for myself.

Acknowledgments

Thanks go out first to my wife, Megan, for her love and support. As well, to my parents, who never said no to two things: books and music lessons. Without them, I would not be doing what I do. A special thank-you goes out to James Ehnes for the insights he was able to impart, all of which made this a much better and more accurate novel. Additional thanks to Will Neises for the use of his name, as well as to all of the kids at Leopold Middle School in Burlington, Iowa, for their continued interest in reading and writing. Thank you, Robin Stevenson, for all your work and assistance with this story. It was greatly appreciated. Finally, I would like to thank all of the kids I have spoken with about music, stage fright and what it means to love playing and performing classical music.

JEFF ROSS is an award-winning author of five novels for young adults. He currently teaches scriptwriting and English at Algonquin College in Ottawa, Ontario, where he lives with his wife and two sons. For more information, visit www.jeffrossbooks.com.